For Jonathan and Jonathan and their flower girl,
Emma Grace, who was worried about the bear
—M.G.G.

KAR-BEN PUBLISHING
A division of Lerner Publishing Group, Inc.
241 First Avenue North
Minneapolis, MN 55401 USA
1-800-4-KARBEN

Website address: www.karben.com

Main body text set in Chauncy Decaf.
Typeface provided by Chank.

Library of Congress Cataloging-in-Publication Data

Names: Gordon, Meryl G., author. | Clifton-Brown, Holly, illustrator.
Title: The flower girl wore celery / by Meryl G. Gordon ; illustrated by Holly Clifton-Brown.
Description: Minneapolis, Minneapolis : Kar-Ben Publishing, [2016] | Series: Life cycle | Summary: "When Emma's cousin Hannah gets married, Emma is thrilled to be the flower girl. However, nothing is quite as she expected it to be, from the ring bearer whom she expected to be a bear, to her celery-colored dress, which she expected to be covered in real celery, to the wedding's two brides"— Provided by publisher.
Identifiers: LCCN 2015040614| ISBN 9781467778442 (lb : alk. paper) | ISBN 9781467778497 (pb : alk. paper) | ISBN 9781512409390 (EB pdf)
Subjects: | CYAC: Weddings—Fiction. | Flower girls—Fiction. | Lesbians—Fiction. | Jews—United States—Fiction.
Classification: LCC PZ7.1.G655 Fl 2016 | DDC [E]—dc23

LC record available at http://lccn.loc.gov/2015040614

Manufactured in the United States of America
1 – CG – 7/15/2016

THE Flower Girl wore Celery

Meryl G. Gordon

Illustrations by
Holly Clifton-Brown

KAR-BEN
PUBLISHING

Emma's dad called her into the kitchen. "Phone call for you, Emma!" It was Emma's grown-up cousin Hannah.

"Alex and I are getting married this summer! Will you be the flower girl at our wedding, Emma?"

Emma loved Hannah, so she said, "Okay!"

Then she thought for a moment. "But Hannah, what's a flower girl?" She imagined herself dressed as a flower.

Hannah laughed. "A flower girl walks down the wedding aisle and scatters flowers on the floor. And she wears a fancy party dress. Can you do that?"

Emma said, "Yes!"

"You'll be great, Emma. Thanks!"

The next day, Emma's father said, "There will be a ring bearer named Jacob at the wedding. He'll carry the wedding rings."

Emma thought for a moment. She imagined a gigantic bear holding rings in his paws.

"Is he very big?" she asked.

"No," her father laughed. "Jacob is your age, and just your size. Maybe you'll dance together at the wedding!"

Emma loved to dance. She closed her eyes and imagined dancing with a bear, just her size.

A week later, Emma's mother said, "The bridesmaids will wear celery dresses. You too! Here's the color." She held up a square of light green satin.

"Will the ring bear wear celery, too?" Emma asked.

"No," said her mother, "he'll wear a black tuxedo."

Emma imagined herself in a light green dress decorated with stalks of celery, dancing with a little bear, just her size, dressed in a tuxedo.

She imagined her cousin Hannah in a beautiful white wedding dress, dancing with . . . who? She didn't remember Alex.

Summer arrived. Emma's flower girl dress came in the mail. Emma watched as her mother unpacked the light green dress. Emma's eyes opened wide.

"But where is the celery?" she demanded.

"What celery?" her mother asked.

"You said the dress would be celery! Where's the celery?"

Emma began to cry.

"Don't cry, Emma!" said her mother. "I didn't know you expected the dress to have celery on it. Celery is the name of this light green color!"

"Oh," whispered Emma. "I don't like celery anyway. I like it better this way."

On the day of the wedding, Emma put on her celery dress and went to the synagogue with her family.

Hannah's mother, Aunt Judy, ran to greet them.

"My, Emma! You look beautiful!" exclaimed Aunt Judy. "Come and meet Jacob."

Emma's heart beat faster. She was going to see the ring bear now!

Aunt Judy took Emma's hand and brought her over to a little boy, just her size, dressed in a tuxedo.

"Emma, this is Jacob. Jacob, this is Emma. You two will walk down the aisle together."

Emma's eyes opened wide. "YOU," she said, "are not a bear! You're just a boy!"

"And YOU," said Jacob, "are not a flower! You're just a girl!"

Aunt Judy laughed and laughed. "Oh, Emma," she said, hugging her. "Jacob is a ring *bearer*, not a bear, because he *bears* the rings. That means he carries them."

"And Jacob," she said, hugging Jacob, "a flower girl is a little girl who carries a basket of flowers. She's not a real flower!"

Emma and Jacob both looked at the floor and scuffed their fancy shoes.

"Look," said Aunt Judy. "Here comes Hannah!"

Emma ran to her cousin Hannah, who was wearing
a wonderful white dress that sparkled in the light.

"How's my favorite
little cousin?" asked
Hannah, picking Emma up
and swinging her around.

Just then another young woman came over. Her dress was white too, and Emma thought it was as pretty as Hannah's.

"Emma, do you remember Alex?" asked Hannah.

Emma's eyes opened wide. She did not remember Alex.

"I'm so happy to see you again, Emma," said Alex, who *did* look very happy.

"Does this mean there are *two* brides?" Emma asked.

"Yes!" said Hannah. "We're going to have a wonderful wedding, especially with you helping! See you inside!" Hannah and Alex clasped hands and hurried away.

Emma thought for a moment. No celery. No bear. And *two* brides! Nothing was what she had imagined.

Jacob came over to stand next to her. "I'm glad you're not a flower. I was afraid I would have to water you if you got thirsty."

Emma giggled.

Emma's mother rushed over. "It's time to start! Here's your flower basket, Emma."

Emma looked inside the basket. It was filled with rose petals.

"As you walk down the aisle, just drop some petals as you go, OK?"

Emma nodded and smiled. This was *exactly* what she had imagined.

Emma and the rest of the wedding party waited behind a door.

Hannah and Alex's grandparents walked down the aisle.

Alex's brothers walked down the aisle.

The bridesmaids in celery-colored dresses walked down the aisle.

Finally it was Emma's and Jacob's turn. Jacob carried two rings pinned on a pillow. Emma carried her flower basket and dropped rose petals down the aisle.

Emma sat with her parents and watched Hannah and Alex walk down the aisle with their parents. Hannah and Alex stood under the wedding canopy. The rabbi read the ketubah and sang seven wedding blessings.

Then Hannah and Alex took the rings from Jacob's pillow. Hannah put a ring on Alex's finger. Alex put a ring on Hannah's finger.

The rabbi put two wine glasses on the floor. Hannah and Alex looked at each other and then stomped on the glasses at the exact same time.

"Mazel Tov!" shouted all the guests as the glasses broke and the musicians began to play.

The two brides smiled and kissed. Then they danced up the aisle. Hannah grabbed Emma's hand and Alex took Jacob's hand, and they all danced into the party room together. The wedding guests clapped and cheered.

It was time to celebrate! Hannah danced with Alex. Aunt Judy danced with Grandpa. Emma's parents danced with each other. Emma danced with Jacob.

The wedding guests lifted the two happy brides in chairs and everybody danced the hora around them, singing and clapping.

At home that night, Emma's father asked, "Did you have fun?"

Emma thought about her celery-colored dress, and Jacob who wasn't a bear, and the two brides with their beautiful dresses and happy smiles.

"Yes," she said. "This was a very good wedding."

"Maybe someday you'll have a wedding," her mother said. "And maybe Hannah and Alex will have a little girl to be your flower girl."

"Or maybe a little boy to be my ring bearer," said Emma.